DOG BREATH

THE HORRIBLE TROUBLE WITH HALLY TOSIS

DAV Pilkey

THE BLUE SKY PRESS
An Imprint of Scholastic Inc.

For Mom and Dad and Halle

The Blue Sky Press

For information regarding permission, please write to:
Permissions Department,
The Blue Sky Press, an imprint of Scholastic Inc.,
557 Broadway New York, New York 10012

The Blue Sky Press is a trademark of Scholastic Inc.

Library of Congress Cataloging-in-Publication Data
Pilkey, Dav, 1966–
Dog breath: the horrible trouble with Hally Tosis / Dav Pilkey.
p.   cm.
Summary: Hally, the Tosis family dog, has such bad breath that Mr. and Mrs. Tosis
plan to give her away, until she proves to be an invaluable watchdog.
ISBN 0-590-47466-9
(1. Dogs — Fiction. 2. Bad breath — Fiction. 3. Humorous stories.)
I. Title.   PZ7.P6314Do   1994   (E) — dc20   93-43405   CIP   AC

24 23 22 21 20   03 04 05
                                                                          49
Printed in Mexico

First printing, October 1994

The illustrations in this book were made using acrylics,
watercolors, pencils, Magic Markers, and Dijon mustard.

Production supervision by Angela Biola
Designed by Dav Pilkey and Kathleen Westray

There once was a dog named Hally,
who lived with the Tosis family.
Hally Tosis was a very good dog,
but she had a big problem.

Hally Tosis had horrible breath.
Whenever Hally Tosis opened her mouth,
horrible things happened.

When the children took Hally Tosis
for a walk, everyone else walked

on the other side of the street.
Even skunks avoided Hally Tosis.

But the real trouble started one day
when Grandma Tosis stopped by
for a cup of tea ...

. . .and Hally jumped up to say hello.

Mr. and Mrs. Tosis were not amused. "Something has to be done about that smelly dog," they said.

The next day, Mr. and Mrs. Tosis decided to find a new home for Hally.

The children knew that the only way they could save their dog was to get rid of her bad breath. So they took Hally Tosis to the top of a mountain that had a breathtaking view.

They hoped that the breathtaking view
would take Hally's breath away...

...but it didn't.

Next, the children took Hally Tosis
to a very exciting movie.

They hoped that all the excitement
would leave Hally breathless . . .

. . . but it didn't.

Finally, the children took Hally
Tosis to a carnival. They hoped
that Hally would lose her breath
on the speedy roller coaster...

FREE BALLOON

Mmmm!
HOT-DOGS!

YOU'LL LOSE YOUR
BREATH

ON OUR
ROLLERCOASTER

...but that idea stunk, too!

The plans to change Hally's bad
breath had failed. Now, only a
miracle could save Hally Tosis.
Sadly, the three friends said
good-night, unaware that a
miracle was just on the horizon.

Later that night, when everyone was sound asleep, two sneaky burglars crept into the Tosis house.
The two burglars were tiptoeing through the dark quiet rooms when suddenly they came upon Hally Tosis.

"Yikes," whispered one burglar. "It's a big, mean, scary dog!"
"Aw, don't be silly," whispered the other burglar.
"That's only a cute, little, fuzzy puppy!"

The two burglars giggled at the sight
of such a friendly little dog.
"That dog couldn't hurt a fly,"
whispered one burglar.
"Come here, poochie poochie!"
whispered the other.
So Hally Tosis came over and gave
the burglars a nice big kiss.

The next morning, the Tosis family awoke
to find two burglars passed out cold
on their living room floor.

It was a miracle!

The Tosis family got a big reward
for turning in the crooks, and soon
Hally Tosis was the most famous
crime-fighting dog in the country.

In the end, Mr. and Mrs. Tosis changed their minds about finding a new home for Hally. They decided to keep their wonderful watchdog after all.

Because life without Hally Tosis
just wouldn't make any *scents!*

Tugboats in Action

Story and photographs
by
Captain Timothy R. Burke

Albert Whitman & Company
Morton Grove, Illinois

The text is set in Avant Garde.
Designed by Sandy Newell.

Text and photos copyright © 1993 by Timothy R. Burke.
Photo on page 6 copyright © 1993 by James Cavanaugh.
Published in 1993 by Albert Whitman & Company,
6340 Oakton, Morton Grove, Illinois 60053-2723.
Published simultaneously in Canada by
General Publishing, Limited, Toronto.
Printed in the United States of America.
10 9 8 7 6 5 4 3 2 1

Library of Congress Cataloging-in-Publication Data
Burke, Timothy R.
Tugboats in action / Timothy R. Burke ;
p. cm.
Summary: A tugboat captain explains some of the jobs done by his boat and others
on the river and in the harbor.
ISBN 0-8075-8112-7
1. Tugboats–Juvenile literature. (I. Tugboats.) I. Title.

VM464.B86 1993   93-9131
387.2'32–dc20   CIP
                                                                                  AC

Shared danger, shared excitement and boredom (I recall one instance of waiting seven hours for a bridge to open), and above all, shared achievement make shipmates special friends. I've learned much from the following tugmen I sail with and wish to express my appreciation for their patience and cooperation throughout the making of this book: Captain M. D. Farrell, Captain H. V. Noonan, W. H. McDowell, W. J. McAndrews, R. J. Hammer, and T. E. Boice.

Kathy Tucker and Judith Mathews, my editors at Albert Whitman & Company, made this book possible. Their early recognition of the value of the topic, then years of encouragement during several revisions, kept the book alive. Book designer Sandy Newell's enthusiasm and artistic and technical abilities get the credit for the superb job of putting everything together.

Heartfelt thanks go to many friends and everyone in my family. Their interest and unwavering faith in my abilities helped this endeavor proceed from an idea to reality.

Timothy R. Burke

This is a Great Lakes harbor tug. A tugboat is a special kind of boat that helps big ships.

Because they are so long, wide, and deep, big ships need help making sharp turns. There are many sharp turns in the narrow Buffalo River leading into Lake Erie. A tugboat, which is small and powerful, can make these turns easily and guide a large ship by pulling it in different directions.

I am the captain. The captain controls the tugboat and tells the crew what to do. I will be sailing the tug down the river to meet a ship in the lake.

But first the crew must ready the tug for action. The deckhand cleans the pilothouse windows. Then he puts life rings in place. I ask another crew member to hose down the deck.

The engineer checks the fuel level, then starts the huge main engine. This one has twelve hundred horsepower. Our tug is strong enough to pull a train! Even though a big ship has its own engine, this extra power helps to handle it.

On the way to the lake, we pass a beautiful blue tugboat pushing a tank barge.

ook! There's a fire tug. She's smothering flames in the ruins of a warehouse with water from high-pressure nozzles.

 ow it's my turn to go to work," I think as a big red ship glides into the harbor.

"She's drawing twenty-three and a half feet," her captain tells me over the radio. That means it's a full load, and the hull of the ship goes down underwater twenty-three and a half feet. She's full of grain from Minnesota and has come here, to Buffalo, New York, to unload.

"Is everything all set below?" I ask my engineer.

"Yes sir," he answers. I have the crew put on life jackets and take their places on deck.

Then I move in to pick up the towline, which will connect the tug to the ship. This maneuver requires a lot of concentration because it can be dangerous. If done improperly, men could be injured or the tug could even be rolled over. Using the tiller to steer and the telegraph to control the speed of the engine, I bring the tug close to the moving ship.

The ship's deckhand tosses a heaving line over to the tug. This light, easily thrown rope is already attached to the heavy towline aboard the ship. My crew grab the heaving line and use it to quickly haul aboard the towline.

My crew work together to secure the towline.

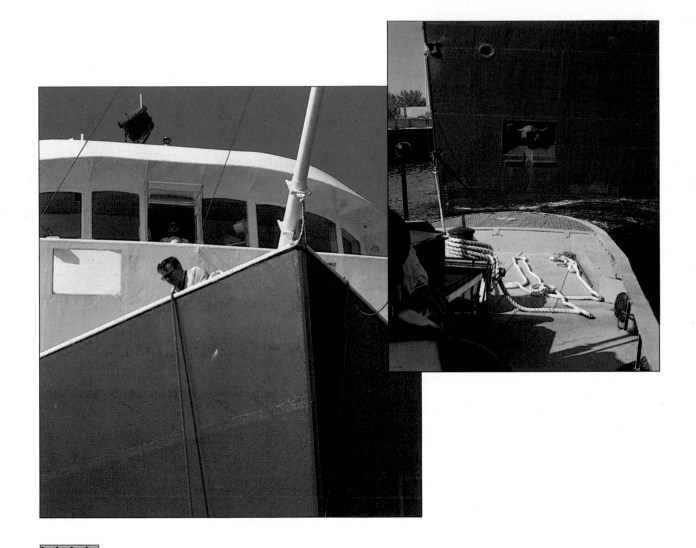

The big ship towers over us as I check her position and my tug's. I see the ship is not following a bend in the river, so I bring the tug way over to the left and pull.

But she's still heading the other way! I push the engine telegraph to Full Ahead.

Finally the ship heads back toward the middle of the river, steering clear of the docked ferryboat we're passing.

Just ahead is a closed lift bridge and beyond it, a sharp bend in the river. I sound the powerful horns to alert the bridge tender and any vessels around the bend.

The bridge tender hears the blasts, stops highway traffic, then raises the bridge to let the tug and ship go through.

Just into the turn, we're faced with a ship docked at a grain elevator. I see her moving ahead, using her mooring cables.

Slowly I tow my ship past the other. I radio the captain of the docked ship to thank him for moving when he heard the horns. This gave us more room to make the turn.

Without warning, our tow veers to the left side of the river. I shove the telegraph to Full Ahead. Our engine roars like a speeding locomotive while the tug's seven-foot propeller seems to make the water boil.

I'm glad I already had the tug over to the right for the next turn; it's hard to tell when river currents may head a ship in the wrong direction. The ship's bow barely misses a rock wall lining the left bank.

I continue the Full Ahead pull and keep the tug at a right angle to the ship. I see progress with each passing minute.

Finally we finish the turn and land the ship at her dock. But she's not close enough to be unloaded, so the ship's captain radios to ask for a push.

At last I hear "up against" over the radio, and stop pushing. Now the ship will be held in position with her mooring cables and winches. Already, sounds of the ship's crew opening hatch covers echo off the grain elevator.

Six hundred fifty thousand bushels of grain will be unloaded within a day. If all this were ground into flour, you'd have enough to make thirty-two million, five hundred thousand loaves of bread!

hat was a good job!" radios the ship's captain as I head toward the tug dock, which is just across the river.

"Thanks for giving us the work, Cap," I reply.

y crew moor the tug by tossing ashore three short hawsers; then they stop the machinery.

We've been gone three hours. I thank my crew for their skillful help. It's been a good morning's work!

More on Great Lakes tugboats

What jobs do Great Lakes tugboats do?

They guide vessels through locks, tow them up and down rivers, and help them dock. They also break ice, helping ships get in and out of harbors during the early spring and winter.

What kind of shipping goes on in the Great Lakes?

About ninety-three Canadian and sixty-nine U.S. freighters crisscross the lakes continually, never leaving the Great Lakes system. They carry millions of tons of grain, iron ore, coal, sand, limestone, and cement between ports. There are also tankers carrying gasoline, heating oil, and liquid asphalt (for road construction).

In addition, four hundred ocean vessels enter and leave the system each year. They bring products from all over the world and sometimes fill up with grain before leaving.

How big are tugboats and the ships they tow?

Harbor tugs are about eighty-five feet long. Ships range from four hundred to one thousand feet in length. A harbor tug weighs about one hundred tons, while a freighter can be twenty thousand tons or more! The ship pictured in this book is 642 feet long.

Tugboats that cross Lakes Superior, Huron, Michigan, Erie, and Ontario are called "outside tugs." They are usually one hundred feet or longer.

Can ships and tugs sail all year long on the Great Lakes?

No. The navigation season begins in late March and ends early in January. During the coldest months of the year, harbor ice is too thick for navigation.

Can tugboats go to work any time of the day in any weather?

Yes! During the season, whenever a tug is needed, the crew will respond in spite of darkness, rain, sleet, or snow.

How many people crew the tug in this book? What does each person do?

There are three: the captain, an engineer, and a deckhand.

The captain navigates the tug, supervises the crew, and fills out logs (written records). Not only must the captain be able to operate the tugboat itself, but he must also be skilled in towing large vessels. The captain needs to be an expert in local knowledge, such as currents, water depths, buoy locations, and hazards.

The engineer starts and monitors (keeps track of) all the engine room machinery and makes sure the tug can do its job. The engineer sounds the fuel tank, checks crankcase oil levels, and does emergency repairs to the main engine. During the tow, the engineer helps the deckhand with line handling.

The deckhand handles lines when docking and undocking the tug and during a tow. At other times, the deckhand helps the engineer with maintenance and repairs.

Glossary

barge–A simple, unpowered vessel which must be towed.

below–Short for "below decks." Any space below the main deck level.

bow–The front of a vessel.

bridge tender–The person in charge of a lift bridge.

current–The flow of water in a certain direction.

deck–The watertight floor that covers the hull.

deckhand–The person who handles lines aboard a vessel and helps with maintenance.

dock–The place where a vessel stays while loading, unloading, or waiting for work.

engine room–The space on a vessel that contains the main engine and many other important pieces of equipment.

ferryboat–A medium-sized vessel that carries people and automobiles short distances.

full ahead–The most powerful position on the engine telegraph. Other positions are *stop, one-quarter, one-half,* and *three-quarters*.

grain elevator–A building where millions of bushels of grain, such as wheat and oats, are kept in tall, cylindrical bins.

hatch–An opening through the main deck that leads to the hold.

hatchcover–A large lid that covers a hatch, keeping the ship watertight and the cargo dry.

hawser–A heavy rope used to tow a ship or moor a tug.

heaving line–A light, easily thrown rope by which a heavier line can be passed from one location to another.

hold–A large inner compartment that contains the ship's cargo.

horsepower–A unit of work roughly equal to the force that one horse exerts in pulling.

hull–The main watertight part of a vessel.

life jacket–A buoyant vest worn to keep a person's head above water if he or she should fall overboard.

life ring–A buoyant ring that can be thrown to someone who has fallen in the water.

lift bridge–A bridge whose main part can be raised to let water traffic pass beneath it.

moor–To fasten a vessel to its dock. Sometimes refers to anchoring a vessel.

mooring cables–Heavy wire ropes used to moor a vessel. Mooring cables are attached to a ship through a winch.

pilothouse–A high, above-deck structure with many windows. The captain navigates from this location.

propeller–The underwater "wheel" with specially shaped blades that moves a vessel when turned by the engine.

radio (or radiotelephone)–A two-way wireless voice communication system that is used between vessels or ship-to-shore.

sail–To navigate a vessel. (We "sail" a ship or tug, even when it has no sails.)

stern–The rear of a vessel.

tank barge–A barge with tanks inside, used to carry liquid cargoes.

telegraph–The device that controls the engine. Using the telegraph, the captain can make a vessel go fast or slow, backwards or forwards.

tiller–The handle or lever used to steer a vessel.

tow–To push or pull a vessel. Or, the vessel a tug is towing.

towline–A special hawser used only for towing.

"up against"–A term used to indicate that a ship's side is against its dock.

vessel–A general term for almost any watercraft.

winch–A power-driven spool that holds mooring cable.